To Andrew from
Miss Sophie
and
Miss Carolyn

12/25/22

This book is lovingly dedicated to my mother, Irene, who started me out with my first pair of white shoes that eventually got "bronzed," only to inevitably be followed by my first pair of White Bucks! The rest is the long path of history.

Papa's Shoes: The Tales of Papa's Life Path

For more information, please contact:
Mascot Books
620 Herndon Parkway #320
Herndon, VA 20170
info@mascotbooks.com

Library of Congress Control Number: 2018910881

CPSIA Code: PRT1118A
ISBN-13: 978-1-64307-299-9

Printed in the United States

The Tales of Papa's Life Path

Written by Michael Oakland

Illustrated by Cameron Grant

On a mid-afternoon day in early winter, Lilikins was over at Papa and Granny's house visiting and her eyes grew heavy.

At her grandfather's suggestion, she went upstairs for some quiet time to perhaps catch a short nap in Papa and Granny's big bed.

It was always so comforting there, so it was very easy to fall asleep, until she thought she heard voices.

Was it Granny and Papa downstairs? No!

Oh my goodness! It sounded like the voices were coming from under the bed! Lilikins woke up just enough to hear them. Who were they? What were they?

Why, they were Papa's shoes all lined up under the bed! Lilikins listened closely as they took turns telling each of their stories about what it was like to be part of Papa's path.

THE MOCCASINS

It was long ago when we would walk silently through the woods with Papa trying not to disturb a thing—not a leaf or a creature.

Simply listening and being present where we were in the light of the moment. Maybe it was a harkening back to the days of Native Americans.

But now, as of late, we're retired to the living room. We slide across oriental rugs and up onto coffee tables while Papa watches television. Life is good!

THE PARTY SNEAKERS

Papa found us by an act of fate, it seemed—we nearly jumped off the rack and into his hands in a small shop in a coastal town in Maine. We felt so out of place there but finally came to life in the heat of summer!

Since then, we make people smile. We're the colors of happiness and we're saved for those special days and nights. And, well, we like it that way. Party on people!

THE LACE-UP BOOTS

We're pretty sure that we've been with Papa the longest of any of you! Since the rock 'n roll days of glory, stages full of music and dancing across the set, steppin' out, and all that equipment we had to haul around. Giant amplifiers, speakers, drums, guitars, and everything else. It was a lot of work and a whole lot of fun. Lace us up! We're ready!

There were nights that we remember, like on a Halloween night under a full moon, we went riding on Papa's black stallion horse, Drambuie. Decked out in steel horse shoes and galloping faster than the wind down the streets and through the neighborhoods all over town. A black cape flying out from behind us, we scared everyone in sight!

We were almost as real as the Headless Horseman, himself, from *The Legend of Sleepy Hollow*. Top that!

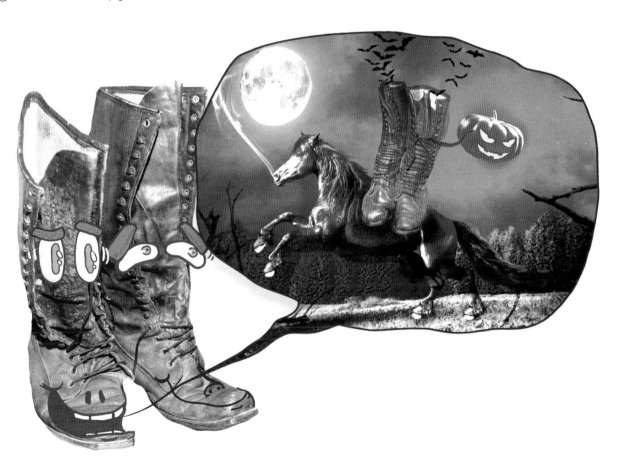

THE DRESS SHOES

Oh my. We've lived such a very different life. I would say that we're right between work and play. Having escorted Papa through many of the finest hotels in the world and across many marble floors and to many gala events. We've passed fountains and tapped the flamenco dancers beat to the sound of Papa's guitar as we shined bright in the evening's light.

The nights would pass gayly as we danced with ladies across the floors, under the stars and beneath the fireworks, on cruise ships and on our way to a midnight refreshment or two with some notable people of interest. This is *the life.*

THE ITALIAN BLONDES

We joined Papa from a fine Italian shoe store in Naples where he paid a hefty price for us, but you do get what you pay for. We, too, like to strike the healthy balance between work and play—we are *loafers* after all.

To be able to travel from Italy to Jamaica and from Napa Valley to Costa Rica in the fairest weather and with the best of company—let's just say we've been Papa's old favorites for a long time now. So long, in fact, that we have been re-soled and re-heeled three times. The cobbler says we're done.

We're tired—it's true. We have traveled many happy miles and it has been a great run, indeed. We're thankful.

THE CLOGS

We helped Papa discover a new part of himself—a casual, cosmopolitan tourist of the world. Flying from Dublin to Montreal, we've walked cobblestone roads and pedestrian malls.

We've danced jigs and done gigs from the Green to the Rocky Mountains, from high upon peaks to the long valleys below... and all in just a wee bit of a heel.

We've sashayed in cafés, drinking espresso and conversing with strangers on important topics. Many moons have passed and, yet, we last as Papa's tried and trues.

From delta dawns to midnight blues, we're some of Papa's favorite shoes!

THE BOAT SHOES

We're really on the back side of all of this. We're the everyday guys—the go-tos—the epitome of the comfort zone. In Papa's world, we're affectionately referred to as the *tropic gypsy shoes*!

Up and down the wharf, the street, the beach, in the boat or the van, flip us off and drive barefoot! We understand. We're good. Casual elegance—that's us! With a nice pair of linen pants, we can go anywhere!

THE BEACH FLATS

Okay, the truth is... we were born in China and made it to the shelves of stores. We've been sculpted by Papa's big toenail from tapping out bossa-nova rhythms in beach cafés.

As fate would have it, one morning when Chef Rita came out of the kitchen, she knelt down before us and put faces on us!

I think that's what started this whole thing. Since then, we've become regionally famous, and have even starred in movies! One was called *Valentine's Day*. We are Julie and Lefty—beat that!

THE WORK BOOTS

Y'all don't even know what work is. We've held Papa steady for years while he worked shoeing horses and blacksmithing. Once, a big ol' draft horse plunked his giant brand new horseshoe right down on us! We just stood there with Papa until he was ready to move it!

Another time, we saved Papa from falling off of a 36-foot ladder leaning on the top of the barn! Better yet, when that chainsaw ripped through one of our cheeks, we saved Papa's toes! Now, *that's* work. That's love. That's what I'm talkin' about!

THE COWBOY BOOTS

We were Papa's *daytime slippers*! That's what he called us. We're made of the finest elk skin from Santa Fe, New Mexico. We didn't come cheap, but we're the best! We've seen it all—rodeos, trick horse riding, and even rattlesnake hunting!

Might I mention that the pretty, young Seniorita Granny fancied us long ago (doing the Boot Scoop Boogie might have helped). We're on our last soles, too. But it sure has been a good run!

THE STRAPPY SANDALS

Well, we just have such a completely different take on all this, fellas. Our scrappy Roman style has caught the eye of a few admirers. No one else here can say that a beautiful lady stopped in her tracks to say, "What beautiful feet you have!" to Papa. We winked!

We have a strength that reveals an inner beauty that is there in comfort and style. That's been our pleasure. If we can sip on a nice beach drink while we're here, well, okay then! Strap us in!

THE FLIP FLOPS

You all have such impressive tales of Papa's life, but we... well, we're really quite chill. We feel no need to go anywhere or be anyone too important. We're just here.

Step in. Don't go too far, or too fast, and everything will be cool. Flip, flop—don't care where we stop. Just don't run backwards!

THE BAREFOOT SHOES

For all of the wonderful paths and the thousands of miles that we've walked and have yet to walk, never forget the best shoes of all... your barefoot shoes! Keep us in the grass or sand, and don't forget to keep a tickle in ya!

Take a walk with someone you love, with or without shoes, making memories and sharing time as our paths intersect.

Thanks be.